MY MUM IS A BANK-ROBBER!

(And other stories)

A collection of short stories for 9-12 year olds

Copyright Cindy Maclean 2016

FOR CHILDREN EVERYWHERE

CONTENTS

CHANGE FOR A PICK-POCKET

Amber were her eyes, just like Amber was her name. Simple as that. Her mother hadn't given that one much thought! It was all part of the same story, thought Amber, as she tucked her straw-blonde hair behind her ears and pushed up her sleeves. The tucking of the hair was the sum-total of Amber's morning hair routine. After all why should she care? Nobody else does; especially not her mother. As a consequence her hair had knots which became like rats' nests if she could hide them for long enough.

Amber was in temporary foster-care, her eighth family to be precise. Seven valiant efforts at trying to make her feel wanted and cared for. She had been too much for them all. Oh they were all perfectly 'nice' people mused Amber as she gave herself a last check in the mirror. Just not 'for her'. Each time the 'nice people' got too close, that is to say that Amber actually started to like them and even feel a little loved, she did something terrible. Really terrible. That's the way she liked it. If her mother didn't want her then she didn't want anybody either. End of.

The truth was that Amber's mum was young, very young to have found herself responsible for a new life; a whole new human being who needed love, attention, milk, clothes, nappies, doctors, sleep, lullabies, books and toys, just to name a few things. Chloe had neither the strength, nor the money, nor the inclination, to give these things. At fifteen she had barely stopped needing some of them herself. The sad fact was she just couldn't do it and knew deep-down in her heart somebody else would do the bringing-up of her own child much better.

Once the decision was made and all the countless meetings were over, it was out of her hands. Chloe enrolled on a Social Care course at the local college and tried to get on with her life as best she could. She wanted more than anything to become a nurse, same as her mum who had passed away a few years before.

Amber knew none of the details of course. All she was told was that her mum couldn't raise her and other people would care for her so much better; give her a better life. She wasn't allowed to know who her real mum was, not until she was eighteen if she wanted to go and find her. Seven years left of other people trying to give her the love she didn't want.

"Ah well," Amber chivvied herself, "at least I have my one good friend, my best friend in the whole world still."

Portia came from a 'well-to-do' family who lived in a house old enough to be covered in ivy and with thin Victorian glass for windows. (Amber could vouch for the glass due to an unfortunate incident with a cricket ball at Portia's birthday party). The house was set on a long, leafy road into the city, only a few miles the other way were the woods and then the Derbyshire moors, both of which they loved to frequent. Portia's house had shutters at the front which tolerated peeling light-blue paint that had seen better days, and a posh, brass door-knocker in the shape of a lion's head, on the sturdy front-door. The door was navy blue. There were stables at the back of this 'mansion', as Amber called it, and Portia was lucky enough to get her brother's hand-me-down ponies.

Portia liked Amber. In fact she admired Amber for her 'don't care' attitude. She personally was never brave enough, and really didn't have the heart anyway, to upset people. Amber liked Portia because she knew that Portia liked her. Genuinely liked her. Together they shared laughs and bike-rides and horsey outings (with Amber running along by Portia's side or trying to keep up on her bike). Their favourite spot to go to was a river-bank where they screamed and made banshee-noises on a rope-swing, laughing until they were weak if the other one fell off. They often waded upstream, one behind the other trawling for frogspawn, blood-worms and 'skaters'. They had spent hours on end together this summer holiday and had never tired of each other's company.

In looks the two girls were polar-opposites, Portia was stocky with dark brown hair which she wore either in a longish, perfectly-cut, perfectly-brushed bob, or in a small ponytail for wearing under her riding hat. Her hair was always, always shiny and smelt of strawberries. Amber was glad to have Portia as her friend, not because of the big house and ponies or any of that, but because they understood each other. Despite their differences in upbringing they knew immediately what the other one was thinking. That made Amber feel safe and comfortable.

Portia's father was French and her mother was from some wealthy place near London. They were laid-back and had a laissez-faire attitude about child-rearing. If Portia was happy then so were they.

One balmy, late August afternoon Amber and Portia were lying idle in their favourite spot by the river.

"I've got something I want to show you!" said Amber suddenly.

She jumped up so fast that her flowery pumps skidded, leaving a heel-mark in the dry mud on the bank. Portia opened one eye wondering what on earth Amber was up to now. Life was never dull when Amber was around! Amber brought over a parcel from the basket on the front of her bike. It was a parcel made from a tea-towel which was bulging with what seemed to be a lot of quite heavy items. She carried it by scrunching the top together, and held one hand underneath to support the weight.

"I'm very curious!" said Portia, "what have you there?"

She sat up now, enthusiastic to share Amber's surprise. Amber knelt down in front of her and laid out the contents of the tea-towel.

"Promise you won't tell? On your life I mean. Swear on your pony's life..."

Amber was staring into Portia's shocked, green eyes, straight into them, hard as steel. Portia didn't break the eye-contact before saying "course!"

The tea-towel was a 'Guide dogs for the Blind' one which belonged to Amber's new foster-Mum and Dad. They both did some charity work for blind people as often as their time allowed around Amber. Whether it was out collecting door-to-door or helping with a 'grow the biggest sunflower' event (as they had this summer – 2.06m the winner, which even impressed Amber!), or running the coffee morning at the local centre. They were always busy doing something for the blind and their guide-dogs.

Apparently her new foster-Dad had a sister who was blind and lived In Australia. He had loads of sisters but this was his way of helping the blind one. She wasn't here, and because he couldn't do anything directly, he would do what he could for the centre. That's what he had told Amber.

On the tea-towel, on top of the picture of the large golden Labrador's head, was what Portia could only describe as 'loot'. Treasures of all-sorts but mainly money, lots of money; five pound notes, two pound coins, 5p's, 20p's, pound coins, even a purple note (twenty pounds!). There was a silver bangle-type bracelet, a gold necklace with a musical note attached, some car-keys, a blue credit card, a wallet in soft, black leather, and a sports-style watch.

Portia looked on with her mouth agape. It took a while for any words to come out. Amber was restless but beaming, waiting for her friend's reaction, still on her knees and desperate to know what she thought.

"What the... what have you been doing Ambs?" stuttered Portia in disbelief.

"I got it for us," replied Amber, a little more sheepish now and suddenly unsure which way this was going to go. Was Portia pleased? She couldn't tell. Portia was her best friend in the whole universe and she just wanted to impress her, to be a worthy friend.

"Ambs you have to get rid of this stuff," Portia said slowly, clearly shocked. She looked around the river-bank for signs of other people in case they should see.

"Seriously Ambs, this is not good, where did you get it all?"

"I sort of took it," confessed Amber, not sure now if she should have been so proud of herself.

"I only took from people who looked posh and wouldn't miss their things. Hippety-hoppety, pickety-pockety!" she grinned, trying to make light of it.

"Anyway," she continued, "they've got loads of stuff that I haven't got, and why should they? What's fair about that? I don't have hardly anything, so I just snatch a bit for myself, out of open handbags or peoples' back-pockets. I keep it all in a box at the bottom of the wardrobe. We can share it 50:50 if you like, you choose first and we'll split the money..."

"Ambs, I don't want any. Take it home. I'll think of what to do," said Portia carefully. "I'll meet you here tomorrow at two o'clock, and without the stuff, or else..."

Amber knew she'd gone too far. She didn't know what to do anymore and did what her friend suggested. The 'loot' had put their friendship at risk, she knew that. All night she tossed and turned, hating what was in the empty shoe-box at the bottom of her wardrobe. It was as if it was burning a hole in the wardrobe door.

Amber hardly slept and the hours wouldn't pass quickly enough, nor the next morning either. Her foster-parents were busy with Saturday morning jobs;

"We should be thinking about the things you'll need for the new term at school Amber you know," suggested her new Mum.

"There's still one more week to go," replied Amber drearily. "Can we think about it after the weekend instead?"

"Sure," agreed her foster-Mum, "but early next week, okay? So you're well-prepared."

The truth was, Amber couldn't think beyond two o'clock today, let alone about next week. What if Portia didn't show? What if she had the police or her parents with her? Amber felt sick. Surely her best friend will help her? She may not have been impressed, but surely Portia wouldn't 'shop' her to the cops or anything, would she? Amber realised that the sick feeling in the pit of her stomach was more about their friendship than anything else. She was used to being in trouble, disappointing people, being rude, selfish and mean. Not to Portia though. She honestly felt she loved Portia more than anyone else in the whole world. Portia understood her, liked her for who she was, despite her being in foster-care and despite the fact that Portia had far more than she did. She would never steal from Portia, never! Amber had a terrible thought; maybe Portia will think that though!

Amber was at the river-bank at ten minutes to 2 o'clock, pacing up and down, kicking twigs and stones with the tip of her pumps to see if she could get them into the river with one 'punt'. Ten minutes felt like ten hours. Finally she saw the shape that was Portia, cycling towards her through the leafy wood, ducking under low branches; dappled sunlight behind her. Portia skidded her bike to a halt but didn't lay it down next to Amber's as usual. She stayed astride and didn't smile. In fact she looked deadly-serious, thought Amber.

"Hi"

"Hi"

"Look Ambs, I've hardly slept a wink and I've been thinking, a lot. Nobody else knows, and I'll still be your friend, but you have to get rid of that stuff. I've got a plan..."

Portia shared her plan with Amber who listened more carefully than she'd ever listened to anyone in her whole life. She fidgeted and kicked the dust, drawing patterns in it with toe of her shoes, but she listened all the same.

"Okay, I'll do it, I promise," said Amber, more cheerfully than she felt.

A week later it was the start of the Autumn term at Westcroft School. Portia and Amber were in the same form at their new secondary school. As they wandered the tennis-courts which were used for break-times, Portia asked Amber if 'everything' was ok. It was the first time they'd had a chance to speak since the unfortunate incident with the money. Portia and her family had taken a last-minute trip to France to visit her father's relations before school started. Amber had been whisked here, there and everywhere to get uniform and all she needed for her new school. She liked her new foster-family, and since spending time with Portia, Amber had come to realise that it's okay to like people and to let them like you. In fact it makes you feel good and she had started to like that feeling. Now she had begun to appreciate that it's a situation that works both ways. Give and take.

"Everything's fine, couldn't be better really," replied Amber happily.

"Look Ambs... I'm sorry if I went a bit weird but I don't want a friend like that... who steals."

"I know, I can see that now, honest I can," agreed Amber.

Amber had heard Portia loud and clear the last time they met at the river-bank. What's more, she was <u>not</u> about to lose her 'bestie'!

"I've posted the wallet 'n' jewellery 'n' stuff to Westcroft Police Station in a carrier-bag wrapped in brown paper," explained Amber. "I used some of the money to pay the postage and the rest I've put in the Guide Dogs for the Blind collection-box in the supermarket. Figured that was a good cause. Forty-eight pounds in all."

"Still friends?" ventured Amber.

"Still friends," smiled Portia.

"Never again, nothing like that ever again. I was so scared you wouldn't be my best friend anymore," Amber confessed, not even recognising the sound of her own voice but liking it very much.

They walked side by side into class.

"So, can anyone tell me what they'd like to do for a job when they're older?" A first PSHE lesson with Miss McDonald...

"Yes Amber? Your hand was up first..."

"I'd really like to be a nurse Miss."

HECTOR FROM SOWETO

"If I don't look up, she won't ask me anything," Hector said to himself. He was staring at his hands, counting the creases on his knuckles as if suddenly that was a very important thing to do. He was also praying, praying that Mrs Jeffries wouldn't ask him a question, which he no doubt wouldn't be able to answer. Then all the class would probably laugh at him, maybe the teacher as well even. This was not going to go well, he could tell that!

Hector's palms were sweaty, he thought they must surely be dripping puddles onto the bright-blue desk-top, and his heart was beating about three million times faster than normal. He felt so ill that he felt he must look paler than the palest white-kid in the class.

Hector was ten years old and had been in England for exactly three weeks, four days, seven hours and twelve minutes. Until three and a half weeks ago he had lived in Soweto, a township on the outskirts of Johannesburg in South Africa. 'Soweto' stands for South-West Township and his family live in one of the little matchbox houses there which make up most of the town. It's a large township with a population of four million, but mostly poor people. Where Hector lives there's a large cemetery, a school, the Soweto hotel, some restaurants, cafés, shops selling sugar, newspapers and bread, and most importantly, around the corner and down the road from Hector's, is the Mandela Museum. This is where Nelson Mandela actually lived. Desmond Tutu lived in the exact same road too, so there were always loads of people visiting the area, bustling around.

Hector grew up in the tiny house with his Mum, Dad and baby sisters. The girls are 5 and 7 years old now but Hector just remembers being told by Mamma to 'watch the babies' if she was popping out. His parents named him Hector after Hector Pieterson. Hector Pieterson was one of the boys who were killed in the Soweto uprising in 1976. This made Hector feel proud of his name.

Hector's Mum had one great-big, bad temper so he always did what he was asked, always. Mostly though he loved to escape the house and play football. He started playing when he was about four years old, kicking a make-shift football around with the older lads. They'd made the ball out of newspaper held together with packing-tape which they had pulled off a cardboard box outside the shop. Hector was truly happy then; chasing and dodging, dribbling and shooting in the red dust, trying to outwit the bigger boys. They all had their own celebration for a goal and would take-off, running around the pitch madly, with their shirt-front pulled up over their head or kissing their 'ring' finger like they'd seen the famous players like Beckham or Rooney do. These boys however, all played in bare-feet and never noticed the heat. Beads of glistening sweat covered their faces and would stay there until a sudden tackle would jolt the beads to the ground. Oh how Hector loved these hours of dusty play. The boys used anything they could for goals at one end of the pitch; usually a couple of cans or someone's pumps, whilst the goal at the other end was always the same. It was painted on the wall in red, just like a proper goal! Quality! The pitch itself? Well that was just a spare piece of ground with a metal fence separating it from the garage next door, but hey it was their pitch and they loved it. Hector wished he was back there.

"Hector, hello, hello! Could you tell me what you think please?"

Oh no! It was the voice of Mrs Jeffries! Hector's mind came back to the classroom he was sitting in faster than the jet plane he had arrived on.

"Sorry Mrs Jeffries, I wasn't listening," admitted Hector honestly. There was a little snicker from a couple of directions in the room, but Hector stayed with it.

"About what please, Mrs Jeffries?"

"About famous footballers, professionals; do you think they are paid too much money?" repeated Mrs Jeffries.

Bingo! Thought Hector. Something I can talk about, give an opinion on, maybe I won't look as stupid as I thought. Here goes...

"I think that if they are good role-models, like Beckham, not like Suarez who bites players, then I think they are something to aspire to."

Hector was proud of his English, he had worked hard at it in his old school in the hope that one day he would use it in England. He was doing exactly that!

"Very good, that's an interesting point Hector, thank-you. And do you agree with Melissa that they work hard for their money?"

Hector hadn't heard Melissa speak, at all, not a word of it, but he decided not to confess a second time.

"Yes, I think they work very hard, training all hours, on special diets and away from home much of the time."

"Thank-you Hector," smiled Mrs Jeffries as a sign she was going to leave him alone now and move on. Strangely though Hector felt he would happily have carried on speaking. The others in the class were quiet while he spoke and hadn't snickered again, he thought they might even actually be interested in what he had to say; Mrs Jeffries seemed to be.

It just so happened that Mrs Jeffries knew perfectly well that Hector was interested in football. She knew he was in England, (in Birmingham), on a scholarship-type arrangement for football and had been training with one of the Aston Villa youth teams over the last few weeks. The other children didn't know this, and Mrs Jeffries had decided not to 'let-on' as it could cause some sort of jealousy or maybe cause Hector to be swamped with questions and be overwhelmed. No, he needed as calm a start to school in England as possible. The children of Class 6J would find out sooner or later in the playground or future lessons, but all in good time.

"The main thing is that Hector settles," she had told his 'host' parents.

Little did he know it himself yet, but Hector was actually a very interesting and exceptional young man. It would take time for him to come to realise this. His love of football, the hot, dusty pitch he used to play on, his older friends there, and Soweto itself, had all added up to him being a great player and a fine young man. Great skills, great fitness, great temperament. Hector knew something of the African players in the Aston Villa mens' squad both past and present and knew that anything was possible. After all, the likes of Hadji and Kachloul (Morocco), Ni Lamptey (Ghana) and Eric Djemba-Djemba (Cameroon) have all come from Africa and played for Villa at some point. In fact Jean Makoun is from Cameroon and is training there now, ready for the start of the 2011 season. As for South Africans like himself; Steven Pienaar has been at Everton since he was there on loan in 2007 (definitely one of Hector's heroes!)

Hector's biggest hero of all time though was Teko Modise, a Sowetan mid-fielder who played for the Orlando Pirates at the Orlando stadium in Soweto. A real 'home boy'. He won SAFA, the South African footballer of the year award in 2007, and 'so' deserved it. If only...

Still, Hector couldn't believe that here he was training at the same club as Jean Makoun and would get plenty of opportunity to watch him train and play. Nothing gets much more amazing than that. Scholarship or not, if he stuck at it, who knows where things could lead?

It all started for him when the Orlando football stadium had been rebuilt and completed the previous year in Soweto. Can you believe that, millions of pounds put into football in his home-town? Hector and his friends thought that if they saved up for long enough they could maybe get to see some of the big matches there! They already hung around the stadium, hoping to get a glimpse of their favourite players. Not only that though, the stadium was able to offer more to schools around Johannesburg and especially in Soweto. Hector's first thought had been that free tickets for a big game might be on the cards, but it actually turned out to be even better than that.

Hector's school was asked for promising footballers to go to a training session at the new stadium. Hector's name was put forward, along with some of the boys he played with out of school. Just a few days before the training session Hector was playing with his friends on the wasteland behind the metal fence. It was the weekend and Hector was determined to prepare himself well for the big school day at the stadium. He was making sure to play his finest football, practising his 'Kreuf-turns', his overhead cycle-kicks and passing his friends on the wing with the speed of the wind. It all came together like a true pro!

"Hey kid!" called a man's voice.

All the players looked over, not sure which one of them 'kid' was referring to.

"Yes, you kid!" A long finger pointed through the fence at Hector. The finger wiggled in his direction so there was no doubt it meant him. Hector ran over, his friends surrounding him at the fence but politely staying behind him.

"You're good! What's your name?"

"Hector, Hector Makola," grinned Hector, pleased with the compliment.

The man, it turned out was Jonno, a coach at the stadium. He had been down the road visiting the Nelson Mandela Museum with some friends of his from England. Jonno asked Hector if he would be attending the school training session on Tuesday at the stadium. Hector told him that 'yes' he had been selected to go. He felt like a million dollars now but wanted to hide that fact from his friends. Of course they teased him mercilessly until they went home for tea.

"Hey I think Jonno needs glasses Hector!" and

"I think Jonno was talking to me, not you Hector, "

were just some of the comments which were followed by a chorus of whooping and laughing. Hector didn't care one bit. These were his true friends deep-down, and there was an unwritten bond between them, which was a kind of 'law' of the game. After-all it was him that Jonno had chosen to talk to. He couldn't be happier!

Hector's Mum and Dad were pleased with his news about Jonno but they didn't really understand how he felt, not really, how could they? His 'baby' sisters weren't in the slightest bit interested. All the same Hector went to sleep that night dreaming.

"Right class! So now I would like you all to chat in your groups about people who you know have worked hard or suffered some hardship to get where they wanted to be, and have succeeded."

It was Mrs Jeffries again.

"We will share the most interesting ones from each group before you go out for break" she explained.

"You have ten minutes 6J!"

Hector's group; four girls and two boys (including himself) scanned each other's faces as if to see who was going to make a move first. After a few seconds one of the girls piped up:

"My Nan worked hard in the war. She drove a land-tank and didn't even have a driving license! She helped this country."

Hector's parents had told him that in the Second World War, the British men had to go away to fight in the army. The women had to do their jobs here at home while they were away, in order to keep the country on its feet. They worked the farms, factories and did the military-type jobs required to keep the country running and so support the war.

Emma, who had friendly eyes and a gap between her teeth, re-did her pony-tail whilst explaining that her Dad was a horse-trainer in Warwickshire. She didn't live with him, but he said that training race-horses was the hardest job in the world, and so she would have to count him into their list of achievers.

"What about Nelson Mandela?" Hector wasn't sure if he should have said this. He didn't know if they would even know who the great man was. Now he might have to explain it all himself, and that would mean the whole group staring at him for ages.

"Oh yes! Brilliant one!" said Emma with the teeth and eyes.

"Yes!" agreed Tom, the boy with glasses on Hector's left.

"Good one Hector; we studied him for our class assembly last summer term," said Tom.

"His house is a museum now, it's actually round the corner and down the road from where I live in Soweto," Hector explained.

"No!", "Omg!" and "That's so cool!" were some of the comments from his group.

Hector was elected by his friends to share his 'person' with the rest of the class. So far it had been a much better morning than he had imagined, and maybe, just maybe, he wasn't as dim or boring as he thought.

Jonno had bounced down the corridor towards them that Tuesday at the stadium. As they sauntered along, Hector and his friends were looking left then right, at the walls which were covered with photos of famous footballers. There were inspirational quotes from players and managers and pictures of World Cup teams as well as individuals, lining the white-washed walls. Of course there were plenty of the home team as well, the Orlando Pirates. It made the boys feel famous themselves for just being there. Jonno greeted them enthusiastically and showed them where to go to change and leave their bags. The boys only had the customary drawstring school pump-bags with them. Hector had nothing in his except for a Match Attack card of an Eastern European footballer he'd never even heard of. Someone in school had given it to him as they didn't want it. Hector hadn't had any to swap and the boy said he could have it anyway. Ah well at least he had that one and was actually a little proud of it. The truth is Hector didn't have any football kit anyway, no boots, no nothing really to keep in his pump-bag. He had the clothes he wore to school, which were the same ones that he wore at home, and the same ones he played football in. A red tee-shirt, black school shorts and black pumps. His Dad didn't have a job and 'the grant' they were given because of that wasn't much for a family of five to live on. Mum stayed at home too, she was always busy though.

Well, Hector didn't care about any of that, not now especially. He was just pleased to be inside the new stadium with his dusty-pitch playing friends around him. It felt more like 'home' than home did! He was soooo excited! Hector was duly selected for the Orlando youth squad along with a couple of his mates. He was selected for his skills and 'tenacity' whatever that meant! They were to attend training each Tuesday evening. There would of course be other boys he didn't know, from other townships and from the city of Johannesburg. Pride did not cover it, and Hector couldn't wait to tell his parents!

"That's great Hector, but we can't afford the kit and the fees you will need for training," was his father's response. Hector explained that the cost would all be taken care of. Part of the deal was that he would be given a new kit with boots, proper football boots, to play on the proper football pitch. The pumps he had played in so far had got him through, but nobody wanted him training in his black lace-up pumps with several eyelets missing, frayed laces and holes in the toes, he told his parents.

"And there won't be any fees Dad," he explained. "It's all part of the new sports training programme sponsored by the government."

Hector went from strength to strength in training and was soon picked for the Orland Pirates 10U's first-team. He was beginning to realise for himself that he might have 'something special ' and when he played at the stadium, he honestly felt like he could walk on water. Jonno talked to his friends in England about his 'special player' and it was arranged for Hector to be given an amazing opportunity. Jonno's friends would 'host' Hector while he attended the Aston Villa training academy next season. The Club was not far from their home in Birmingham. Jonno sorted the funding and from then on it all happened very quickly. Hector's parents had agreed and so here he was. Jonno had travelled with Hector from Johannesburg, changing planes in Algeria for the next 'leg' of the journey to the UK. Jonno stayed with his English friends along with Hector and took his young superstar to meet the Villa staff at the ground. Work in Soweto had since called him back to South Africa, but before leaving, Jonno told Hector that he had absolute faith in him as a footballer and to make the most of this opportunity.

"Make the very best of it Hector," were Jonno's last words to him.

From being the quiet, shy boy who didn't dare speak in class, Hector became like a National treasure! The children of 6J loved his stories of Soweto, which amazed them. Mrs Jeffries knew he added to the richness of the class. He was often surrounded at break-times by a group of friends who hung on the end of every one of his words. That's of course before he excused himself modestly and politely to go to play some football.

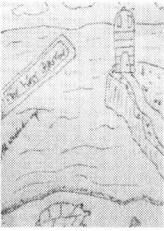

ALL WASHED-UP

"Giant Leatherback turtle found dead on Falmouth beach!" was the headline in the West Briton newspaper.

Underneath, the article continued:

"This is such a shame to see" said Joy Tresidder, a Marine Conservation Biologist. "The Leatherback is an endangered species. This turtle probably lost its way whilst hunting for jellyfish, as it is generally native to the Caribbean, four thousand miles away! It appears to have died from swallowing a plastic carrier-bag out in the bay which it obviously mistook for food. The turtle will most likely have choked but we are running further tests to check if this theory is correct. It is important that we know exactly what has happened to him."

Marsha's blood ran cold. She loved animals and it pained her to think of people hurting them in any way. She was always glued to those RSPCA programmes, especially the ones about dogs. It made her so angry though, and she would call out "stupid idiots!" at the people who were caught mistreating their pets. She wanted them to hear her through the television.

"Marsha!" her Gran would say, telling her off for her bad language, but at the same time Marsha knew that her Gran agreed.

"Well it's true Gran, they are stupid and they shouldn't be allowed to keep animals if they can't look after them properly."

Gran would look at Marsha from over the top of her glasses and smile. She really was such a dear girl and something to be proud of, what with Marsha growing up with her own hardships and all.

Marsha had turned twelve that year, at Easter actually. It was never a very happy time for her anymore though. Her birthday fell just a few days before the anniversary of the worst day of her life; the day she lost both her parents. Gran had never questioned the idea that Marsha would live with her, after all it was her own daughter's flesh and blood.

Marsha remembered the date-March 29th, better than her own birthday on the 25th. She had been close to her Gran before, but now she had lost her parents, they were 'stuck together', inseparable.

Gran's name was Violet, Violet Roswell. She was born in Fowey, a little town not far from St. Austell in Cornwall. It's pronounced 'Foy' and is one of the prettiest places you could ever visit. It has a small picture-postcard harbour, row upon row of twee terraced houses which run along the Esplanade, most having their own special name painted on a slate or drift-wood sign outside the front door. There is a gorgeous little town-centre filled with interesting shops and coffeehouses.

Violet worked in a bakery there as soon as she left school and was known for making the best Saffron buns. She married Jowan Trudgeon as soon as he asked, and moved away with him. Jowan worked at the dockyard in Falmouth and Violet moved into the small house that came with his job. Old-man Jowan had sadly died five years ago and so it was a sort of mixed blessing when Marsha moved in. They were meant for each other, after a series of devastatingly sad losses she and her Gran were a 'port in a storm' for each other, and it had to be said that they rubbed along together very nicely.

Nowadays Violet was in the habit of rising early each morning, and walking briskly to the local shop for some fresh- air, a newspaper and two Saffron buns. The shop was one of only a few where they lived, on the outskirts of town, and consequently it sold most things. It had its own post-office section, newsagents, bakery and was also a hardware store; all in one shop.

Violet always made sure to pop a Saffron bun into Marsha's schoolbag for her to have at break-time. They were both fond of them and Violet thought this must be in the Cornish family genes. This morning Violet had returned from her sunny morning walk, full of the joys of Spring (despite it being July), but she knew instinctively that Marsha was not going to be happy. She unfolded the newspaper and left it on Marsha's side of the breakfast table, covering her yet to be used cereal bowl.

That's when Marsha came downstairs and read the headline about the turtle.

"Gran, can I take the newspaper to school with me please?"

"Of course" said Violet, "I've read it already... well the bits of it I wanted to read anyway. You take it sweetheart."

Marsha knew she had Biology today. She also knew that Mr Tench would be very interested in this news. Second lesson couldn't come fast enough for Marsha. Then, all through the lesson she could almost feel the heat from the article burning a hole in her school rucksack, beseeching her to get it out. "It must be warming up that Saffron bun", Marsha smiled to herself, amused at her own little joke. She struggled hard to concentrate on what Mr Tench was saying about animal cells and chromosomes. Interested as she was, there was something much more important for her to talk to him about. In fact Marsha would have liked the rest of the class to magically disappear so she could have Mr Tench's attention all to herself, to tell him about the Leatherback turtle.

Finally the school bell rang for the end of the lesson, and so for break. A good time to catch Mr Tench.

"Sir, have you seen this?" Marsha asked, fumbling around with her rucksack zips and brandishing the newspaper towards her teacher.

"Indeed I have Marsha! I read it in the staffroom this morning before school. Dreadful, just dreadful. A crime against wildlife, shocking!"

Marsha knew he would have an opinion on the matter, being a Biologist himself. His reaction was a mixture of sadness at the tragedy, tinged with a certain amount of pleasure at Marsha's interest in the matter.

"Well I was thinking Sir, maybe we could do something about this..."

"I'm delighted to hear that young lady! I'm on break-duty Marsha so I have to dash but you give it some thought and maybe you could run some ideas by the class next lesson?"

"Yes Sir, definitely. Yes I would like that very much!"

Mr Tench shot out of the door. Marsha had been given the green-light! The green-light to do some good for the sake of animals. Not just for animals, for an endangered species. She was about to change the world in her own small way.

Marsha ran ahead of her friends after school.

"Hey Marsha! What's with you then? What's up Marsh?"

Marsha hadn't time though. Time was definitely of the essence now. Next Biology lesson with Mr Tench was on Friday and today was Wednesday and she had some research to do. Striding out like a power-walker on a treadmill, she made quick time of the lanes along to home. She burst in the back-door:

"Hi Gran! Sorry, I have to do some work on the turtles for Mr Tench! He was really sad but pleased... class next lesson... the others could help..." Marsha's voice trailed off and then there was silence as she closed her bedroom door.

"Well she's fired up about something!" Violet said to herself, smiling.

Two hours later Marsha appeared downstairs for tea. Gran had laid out the table with cutlery and the usual green plates that had three grooves circling the outer edge, and which used to belong to Violet's Mum. There was sea-salt in a bright-blue 'Saxa' container and the wooden pepper-grinder which Marsha had given Gran last Christmas, but neither of them used. It was just nice that it was always there as a reminder, and it looked posh after all, thought Marsha. Violet always put the grinder out to let Marsha know she liked it and that she hadn't wasted her money. All this was laid on top of a cheery yellow table-cloth patterned with blue forget-me-nots. There was a dish on the table with cheese-pie in it, piping hot, and Gran had already spooned some baked beans out onto each of their plates.

"Oo yum! My favourite!" Marsha exclaimed on seeing the mash covered in melted cheese. She licked her lips in anticipation and pulled her chair in under her with a few short chugs. Gran passed her a large serving-spoon.

"Mr Tench said I can talk to the class next lesson about the Giant Leatherback they found on the beach. He saw it in the paper too, and he's keen to hear any ideas I have about how to help them. They're an endangered species you know Gran."

"Yes I read that too," said Violet. She was so proud of Marsha, it made her feel like her heart would burst right out of her chest sometimes.

She was a smart girl too thought Violet. Not brilliantly clever but clever enough to know right and wrong, and to have this amazing desire to put ideas into action. She had come so far.

"Who else has seen rubbish floating around in the bay?"

Marsha was standing in front of the class on Friday. She was really nervous but knew that she had to do this now. It was serious, no more lives should be lost in the Leatherback species and definitely not if she could help it. Marsha was surer of what she was doing than anything she had ever done in her life. Her classmates agreed to having seen rubbish in the sea; tin-cans, fishing-line, plastic bags and such, floating around. Marsha showed them the news article and explained what it said in case they hadn't already seen it.

"The turtle died because of a carrier-bag in the water and they've confirmed that now," explained Marsha, "and I have an idea to share with you... I'll need help with it though," she went on enthusiastically.

"If it can happen to turtles then it could happen to seals and other sea life."

Marsha asked for volunteers to help with her campaign. They were to sign-up at the end of the lesson if they were interested in working on her idea with her. Twelve people signed up, plus Mr Tench himself. Not only was he keen to help but he suggested he may be able to swing any financial costs with the Parents' Association and the Head teacher.

Six months later, after much advertising; posters, leaflets, school assembly and letters home, there wasn't a soul in the local area that didn't know of the campaign 'Save our Sea life'.

Marsha had, along with some of her team, given the Parents' Association a short presentation also. And this was the best part of all; the team had explained to them about the supposedly 'bio-degradable' carrier-bags at supermarkets, which 'yes', were improved now, and granted, the extra cost was putting people off having to buy them, but they were still a risk, if dumped in the sea. They took many years to decompose. Wildlife could still get tangled up in them and even choke like the Leatherback had, before the bags disintegrated. Marsha had used her pocket-money to invest in a 'turtle bag' to show the Association. She had seen them online on her computer when she was doing her research and they came in attractive colours; bright-blue, yellow, purple and red. The article said they were:

"Totally bio-degradable and break down in the sea very quickly. Most importantly, they are strong, string-like, and are therefore re-usable, so no need at all for nasty plastic carrier-bags."

The PA agreed to give Marsha's campaign enough money to invest in a hundred turtle-bags, which she quickly did with the help of Mr Tench. She then visited shops and supermarkets in the area to gain their support, leaving them with a sample turtle-bag and a letter of explanation on the proviso that she would return for the bag and see the manager in a week's time. She sold the rest of the bags to parents and teachers in school.

The outcome of the story, you are wondering? Well, the supermarkets and shops now re-order their own turtle-bags to sell to the public; locals and holiday-makers alike. They even have their own posters explaining the bio-degradable and re-usable bit. Better than that though, Marsha is now, at twenty years old, a campaigner for Greenpeace and is currently somewhere around the Southern Oceans. She is making sure endangered whales aren't stolen from the sea by people in large ships dishonestly claiming to have permission to use the whales for Science research.

TO BEE OR NOT TO BEE

I used to think that anything that buzzed around was going to sting me and it would hurt. I couldn't see any point in creatures that stung, and I didn't know that they had any sort of 'point' in life. Then I learnt that wasps (not just bees) do actually pollinate some trees, like the fig-fruit wasp which has an incredible life-cycle story. The male is blind and waits inside the fig for a mate to come along. He has no wings as he doesn't go anywhere.

Then I started to find out more about bees and how, without them, we would all probably die. They are sooooo important!

'No bees' means little cross-pollination which means less plants, less trees, less food and oxygen! Get my drift?

Jess's Story

Jess was waiting for her Mum to pick her up from school.

"Late again, she's always blummin' late."

Jess was sitting on an extremely sharp-edged, red-brick wall, grumbling to herself. It was the kind of wall with edges that cut into the back of your legs as you sit, so you have to keep the weight off by sitting on your hands. If you don't, it just hurts too much. Mind, it was better than standing there like a lemon!

Jess had been to Science Club after school. She actually didn't like Science much, she would rather go to Gym Club every night or Athletics Club, but tonight was Science and her Mum made her go. She made her go because she worked until 5pm every day and there was no-one home to look after Jess. So, every night a different club because that's what the school offered. Half past three 'til half-four and then a saunter to the loo before dawdling to the wall, just inside the school gates, at the top of the drive. She wasn't allowed beyond the school gates, her Mum insisted, even though Year 6's were actually allowed to walk home without permission.

So, here she sat, waiting. Bored. Her friends long-gone. They were the saving-grace about having to go to Science Club, at least she had some good company. It could be worse. She could be with 'all boys', or the really geeky group of girls who were much smarter than her and knew what they were doing. At least her friends made it bearable, Jess thought. She shifted on her hands; she'd have red marks at the very least if her Mum didn't get here soon, her legs would probably be cut in half more likely, through to the bone. Her Mum would only have herself to blame for an impromptu trip to the hospital to get her legs sewn back on. Although her Mum probably wouldn't have the time for that!

As Jess sat there feeling sorry for herself, she noticed something fall to the ground. The trees behind her were leafy and green from the summer still, as it was only early September. Nonetheless Jess assumed it was indeed a small leaf blown down from the row of trees behind the fence she was leaning back on. There were gardens behind her, she knew that because the school caretaker lived in one of the houses. Jess had seen Mr Swift disappear several times through a padlocked gate which backed onto the playground a bit further up. She hopped off the wall, careful not to scrape the backs of her legs and went to get a closer look at the mystery object. Jess put her schoolbag down on the ground and inched closer. It soon became clear that the fallen object was actually a bee. It was obviously exhausted and as it lay there, Jess could see it's little body panting. It looked so wrong on the hard, grey concrete, this beautiful thing of flight reduced to a panting mess on the floor. She didn't quite know what to do and didn't want to miss her Mum who was about to come flying up the school-drive like the emergency services themselves. She might think Jess had set off walking home against her instructions if Jess was to go anywhere.

Here Jess was though; responsible for a life, and it really was beginning to look like a life and death situation where every second was going to count.

"Bee-woman to the rescue!" she told the bee. "Don't move a muscle-I'll be right back!"

Jess scooped up her satchel, and with it jiggling on her shoulder, headed back into school. She knew there would be someone in the staffroom, marking books or whatever else they do, if Miss Peters the Science Club teacher was not in her room. She checked for Miss Peters first and 'hoorah!' she was still there tidying up from Science Club.

"Miss! Oh thank goodness! Miss, you have to come quick!" Jess turned and led the way, both of them running, although Miss Peters wasn't quite sure where they were running to; an injured child perhaps? A car-crash? It was clearly going to be something bad judging by Jess's panic.

"There Miss!" pointed Jess as they reached the spot where the tragedy was taking place.

"It's, it's dying Miss, what shall we do with it?"

"Oh Jess!" said Miss Peters in a very smiley, very sympathetic way. "You're a good person! You wait here with the bee. I'll be right back - two minutes!"

One minute and 50 seconds later Miss Peters returned with a little cup of water and a teaspoon.

"Sugar dissolved in water," she told Jess as she wheedled the small spoon of liquid into a position for the bee to be able to drink. Jess watched intently with her fingers crossed, willing the bee to get better.

"There" said Miss Peters, "That's all we can do for her now, apart from hope, we'll just have to wait and see."

They waited.

As Jess's Mum walked round the corner the bee suddenly took flight, straight towards her. It hadn't quite got its bearings and Mum ducked to avoid it. Jess and Miss Peters laughed, partly through amusement and partly through relief.

The week passed rather uneventfully, with Jess settling into the new but last Autumn term for her at Hall Street primary school. They were top of the school now, 'an example to the rest etc., etc.', was the message given to all in Year 6. Jess had enjoyed primary school and she was so familiar now, with the school and the staff that it felt like home to her. She loved the responsibility of Year 6 and jumped at the chance to be on the School Council. She had previously not been keen but this year, thought Jess, this would be her year. She was even going to give Science Club her best shot.

 It wasn't long before Tuesday came around again and Jess was making her way to Miss Peters' room. She was feeling a little less confident than last week because one of her best friends Jemma was off school ill. Ella and Marie were still going but they usually stuck together if there was work to be done in pairs.

"Never mind, best foot forward," Jess rallied herself. She half-wondered if Miss Peters might mention the bee incident last week, but she guessed not.

On entering the classroom, Jess, Ella and Marie quickly found their seats from last week, over by the fish tank. The two goldfish, Miley and Cyrus, seemed to pay even less attention to lessons than they did!

"Well, hello everyone!" greeted Miss Peters.

"Hello Miss Peters," was the general chorus, in reply.

"I thought we would do something a little bit different this afternoon," she continued, "and I think Jess may be interested in today's topic!"

Jess's ears pricked up at this. What on earth could she be referring to? Unless it was the bee incident? She felt a bit panicky all the same.

"We are going to have a debate. About... well perhaps you can work it out?"

With that Miss Peters pressed the Overhead Projector button and it sprung to life, the picture of Richard Hammond appearing pixel by pixel.

"Ah he's cool" someone said.

And "great, Top Gear!" said another, whose group were getting positively excited.

Richard Hammond was standing in full bee-keeping regalia; white jumpsuit with a mesh-fronted hood, white boots and white gloves, with a chirpy grin on his face. He was about to take us inside a hive and show us the 'World of the Honeybee,' and it was fascinating, more like an industry really. Every bee has a job which is decided when the bees are pupae. Whatever temperature they are kept at by the 'heater-bees' dictates whether they will grow to be a housekeeper or forager. The Queen bee is just that, a Queen; there is only one in a colony of around 50,000 bees, 300 of which are usually drones (males), and the rest female worker bees. She is produced from an egg identical to the rest of the bees, but what makes her different is that she is 'chosen' as having potential, and consequently fed a substance called 'royal jelly'.

"Oh my goodness!" said Ella whilst still staring at the whiteboard.

The next clip was about the medicinal properties of bee-stings and how they can be used to ease the pain of rheumatism. Lastly came a report on 'bbc.co.uk/science and nature' about the amount of food we get from the cross-pollination deeds of bees.

"Okay class, so 'to bee or not to bee? That is the question', to quote Shakespeare!" Miss Peters threw out the question as she scanned the room eye-contacting them all in turn.

She continued:

"It's been in the news recently that more and more people are keeping bees in hives on their property. Not just in country gardens either, but on rooftops in London. Some hives are also being stolen! If the Queen bee is taken away, then the rest of the hive will probably follow.

So this half of the class, good things about keeping bees and the other half of the class what are the downsides, the disadvantages? Chat together with your group and then we'll have a debate over whether it's a good thing to keep bees or not. Off you go!"

A lively and interesting debate followed, the downsides had been harder to think of, said that group, but mostly involved being stung and so of course, the risk of anaphylactic attack for those with extreme allergies. Cost, was another consideration, not just of the hive structure and cost of the bees themselves, but clothing as well. They found out that a Queen bee alone can be bought for upwards of thirty pounds they said. A whole colony of bees, over a hundred pounds. Plus they didn't fancy having a robber in their garden!

Jess and her side of the class were the victors however, probably unfairly, as it was clear to see from the video clips that bees are a good thing and even crucial to our very existence.

"And by the way class, you may want to take a leaf out of Jess's book and actually save a bee sometime!"

Everyone looked at Jess who blushed and then smiled.

"That was the best Science lesson everrrr," Jess told her Mum when she picked her up, (actually on-time as well). Her Mum was pleasantly surprised by Jess's new enthusiasm but had news for her all the same:

"Oh, well I was just going to say that I've changed my work-hours on Tuesday now, so you don't have to go to Science Club if you don't want."

"You're kidding aren't you?" was the reply.

So, that was how Jess discovered a love of bees. "Each to their own," you might be thinking, but if something gets you really motivated, then you should follow it. There's nothing better than having a career that you love; ask someone who doesn't enjoy their job!

Jess followed bees into a career. She now works in a laboratory in Southampton as a researcher into bee behaviour and associated diseases. At present she is working on why bees get sick from the varroa mite and the consequent 'hive-collapse' that can follow. If bees get sick they cannot forage for food or find their way back to the hive with nectar. Neither can they perform their little 'bee-dance' which signals a good place to forage for pollen and nectar to other worker bees. If the Queen herself gets sick, the whole hive fails until they nominate and hatch a new Queen. The varroa mite, to the honeybee, is the same size a plate would be on us.

In a recent television interview on the local evening news, Jess spoke of the UK having to import healthy bees from New Zealand, such is the crisis.

The bee that fell to the ground at Jess's feet was responsible for a lot of good work around their future existence.

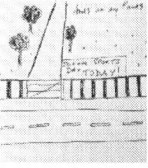

ANTS IN MY PANTS!

When you come from a big family like I do, it's easy to feel like you're last in line. I'm a middle child as well, three older than me, three younger. That means I have to wait for Mum to finish seeing to the little ones before she can even look at me. Asking her a question is a non-starter if she's changing the twins' nappies, bathing Arthur or getting dinner ready. She's always, always busy. The older ones need 'important' things for their 'very important' school-work, exams, Scouts etc., etc. or they need lifts home late when it's too dark to get a bus. Sometimes we all have to go out to get them as Dad's working late and leaves us the car. Mum says she'd much rather go out to work than work at home bringing up kids. She says it must be so much easier.

The older ones; Meg, Dan and Steven are more able to help than me as well, but they never do. Short of cleaning their infested rooms once a month and occasionally helping to bring the shopping in from the car, that's it! So, who cops for it? Yes, me! That's right, if it's doable I have to do it. If it's not, it gets left for Dad to do when he gets home. It's probably why I'm such a pain in school to be quite frank with you. I mean I know why I play-up, I just honestly can't help it. It's like suddenly I have lots of people around me who think I'm funny, crazy, entertaining and are quite happy to give me their attention. It's as if I'm on the telly or I'm a pop-star or something, and what's more, if there's anything I can tap, oh yes boy, I'll tap it. I heard from the woman that talks to me about stuff at home; the family support-counsellor she's called, well she's called Annette really, but anyway, she said that it can cause kids like me real physical pain to have to be still and sit on their bums all the time. So, see, it's an actual fact

My teacher, Mrs Albright, is fabarooney. She has this really cool idea that if I'm going to fiddle with things then she'll give me something to fiddle with. Usually it's blue-tack and that feels soooo good! It's like all my twitches and worries travel through my body to my fingers and get kneaded out into the elasticity of the blue-tack. Then I pretend I'm folding them all up inside it and I can squash them. Mrs Albright also says "Josh, if you need to get off your chair then ask Miss Dunbar." Miss Dunbar is our class TA who is also ace.

"She can tell you when it's a good time to get up and have a wander."

Wandering means the ants go out of my pants for a while and that's so nice.

"I can only help you though Josh if you show us all respect and follow the rules." Says Mrs Albright.

Seams fair. Not always possible though for me I'm afraid. Well, especially one day it wasn't. I try so hard, I really do. I try to do what Miss says cos I like her, and she wants what's best for me and the class, I know that. It just really wasn't my fault, honest!

It was on Sports Day last year. One of my better things is running, as you can imagine, for a person who can't keep still. I take something called Ritalin; one pill every morning and one at night, which helps me to stay more calm. I was in a rush, excited and so a little forgetful on that sunny morning. I remember it being sunny because Mrs Albright had said "if you wake up in the morning and it's raining, Sports Day will be cancelled class. Make sure your parents check their 'phones for a text message from the school. They can always 'phone the school office if they can't get e-mails or texts."

Joy of all joys though, it was sunny, and I couldn't wait! It was of course the usual struggle for Mum getting out of the house, with double-buggy, drinks containers, spare nappies, soothers, sudocreme, spare clothes (in case of the obvious happening at nursery), all packed into two separate bags for the twins. It always looks like we're going on an expedition to the Outback or the North Pole, not walking to school. The older brigade have always long-gone, meeting friends on the corner, or calling at their house for a more grown-up, chatty walk to school. Lucky things.

So, in all the chaos, Mum forgot to remind me about my pill. Never a good thing. It was later on, when I was feeling a bit too excited, a bit too friendly, a bit too up and down, on edge and fidgety that the realization came, that I hadn't taken it. That's what I mean when I say it wasn't my fault.

There was an excited feeling in the classroom when we all sat down for the register. Already I could feel it happening though, some of the, (mostly) boys, but some girls too, were winding me up.

"Hey Josh! Don't run the wrong way in the race, will you?"

And...

"I could run faster than you Josh with my legs tied together!"

And...

"Is your Mum coming to watch you lose Josh?"

All just trying to wind me up and get me going. Mrs Albright tried to stop this stupid stuff by saying:

"It's a Sports Day class, and that means sporting behaviour, which this is absolutely not! Now, show how mature you all are please."

It was too late though, all that teasing I could maybe have dealt with another day, but this one day it was all too much. I was beginning to realise this, and was about to tell Mrs Albright about my pill but I thought she might stop me taking part in the race. So I didn't.

Miss Dunbar came over. She had been sorting out the bags and Home-school books, checking for important messages. I'd forgotten mine, needless to say, along with my medication. Usually Mum was quite good with the Home-school book; it helped if she told Miss Dunbar and Mrs Albright how I'd been at home.

"You're looking a bit stressed Josh, is everything ok?" Miss Dunbar asked.

"They've been teasing me Miss, about the Sports Day." I told her. I pointed to a few of the culprits, who looked away, smiling.

"Just ignore them Josh, you know you're better than that."

Today though, I doubted it. I was upset now, frustrated and seething.

"You should be more supportive boys," he heard Miss Dunbar say to Jake and Ben on her way to the door.

"One table at a time need to go and get their PE kit from the cloakroom," announced Miss Dunbar. "'Kenzuke's Kingdom' first; they look nice and ready! Then we'll have 'Long Way Home'. 'War Horse' aren't ready, I can see that!"

Our table-groups all had the name of a Michael Morpurgo story. We were given a chance at the start of term to think of our own names. Ours is a 'lively' class though, which is teacher-speak for 'too noisy'. So with too much argument and messing around going on, over what should have been a simple task, Mrs Albright just gave us all a name, and that was the end of it. She said that maybe later in the year, if we were all a little more sensible, we could go back to naming the tables ourselves.

I was on 'Long Way Home' table, and Jake and Ben were on 'War Horse', so I got to go ahead of them to find my PE kit. I gave them a triumphant smile as I 'beamed' passed them. They just looked at each other and kept their heads down, hoping that with their folded arms and quiet mouths, that they would be called next.

"Right let's have 'Muck and Magic' next!" trilled Miss Dunbar in the high voice she used for calling out groups.

"'War Horse', I'm still waiting for quiet!"

Finally, everyone was ready.

"I don't know why everything takes so long, "said Mrs Albright.

"Neither do I Miss", I agreed, and Jake pulled a sort of baby-face at me.

The class were given the usual sort of reminders of what Mrs Albright expected; trying our best, sporting behaviour and to remember that there would be parents and other visitors around.

The problem was that I felt like one of those saucepans with the tight lid and a hole in the top. When the pressure builds up inside, steam comes out of the hole. I didn't feel the steam coming out though. Just pressure. Just anger and annoyance which was mostly because of Jake. Jake was definitely going to 'get it'.

Obviously Miss Dunbar needed to be mostly with me during Sports Day, but she told me that she might have to go and help somewhere else, if she was called upon. We had to watch all the younger kids first, and clap them when they finished their various races. A lot of them dropped things; beanbags, hard-boiled eggs etc. They fell over and even bumped into each other, but we still had to clap, all of them, right 'til the very last person finished, and that took ages. All I wanted to do was be in all the races myself. All of them. Now.

I was fidgeting so badly and there wasn't much space where we were sitting cross-legged on our small area of grass. So it was easy to accidentally catch your foot or your knee on the person in front.

"Ow, Josh!" screeched Mona, whose back I had just interfered with.

"Watch-it Josh!" she snarled and then turned back to watch the races.

It was so boring waiting. So hard. Miss Dunbar had swapped herself for a piece of blue-tack, which she left me with, but I guess that was just a drop in the ocean really, compared to what I was really needing. It didn't even begin to calm my super-charged feelings. I twisted it and snapped it in my fingers. I wrapped it round them and then slid it off, I twisted it and snapped it again.

"Class 6A next!" announced Mr Derbyshire, our Deputy Head, over the loud-speaker system.

There were three races for our class. One for the faster runners, one for the least-fast, and one for the in-betweeners. Hallelujah! At last! (I was in the fast race). I couldn't see Mum anywhere as I searched the crowd of

37

expectant parents with my quick eyes. One more thing gone wrong on a day I wanted to shine and show everyone that I wasn't just a silly show-off.

"I am useful at something, I'll show them", I thought.

Jake shoved me in the back; "out the way small-fry!"

"You're just a show-off Josh. All mouth and no action. My Dad says so!" added Jake's side-kick Ben, making his hand 'pretend-talk' in my face as he went past.

"What you going to do when you lose Josh? Cry? Run to Mummy? But wait, Mummy's not here is she, diddums!" Jake taunted.

That was it! I could stand no more. Quick as a flash I was on Ben's back, riding him like he was a donkey and using my weight to shove him to the floor. One down! So next Jake, the cowardly bully. Jake tried to make a run for it when he saw his stupid puppy of a friend felled. Now he would see that I was faster! I legged it after him and he was checking over his shoulder, left and right behind him as he tried to dodge me. I threw myself at his legs like a World-class rugby star and grabbed his foot. Jake fell flat on his face and I could see the blood coming from his nose as he rolled over. I so wanted to punch him in the face but someone had caught my arm as I pulled it back to deliver.

"Josh! Josh! Stop! Appealed Miss Dunbar. "Calm down Josh, calm down! It's okay. Just stand up, hold my hand and take deep breaths," she instructed.

I was crying now, not from sadness but from anger and frustration... from them spoiling my day. I was surely going to get into big trouble now and we hadn't even had the race.

Miss Dunbar led me inside while other teachers and parents helped Ben and Jake. Ben was looking concerned for his friend as someone pulled Jake to his feet and put their arm round him. That's the last I saw as I disappeared inside the school where at least I had shade, coolness and the calm, reassuring voice of Miss Dunbar.

"Miss I didn't have my pill this morning. I didn't say cos I thought I wouldn't be allowed to do the race", I confessed.

"Oh Josh, you should have told us." Miss Dunbar looked at me with eyes that were sort of telling me off, but were still kind. She liked me a lot, I knew this and I felt bad for letting her down, as well as Mrs Albright and the school, and my Mum. 'Oh no! She'll tell Dad and it will be just as bad again later, as it has been today', was the thought that came into my mind.

The outcome of all this?

Well, let me tell you:

I have taken on more responsibility now. The twins are a bit older and less of a struggle for Mum. I'm the one that remembers my medication and remind Mum, because I know the consequences for me if I don't. The best part is that I'm seeing a behaviour therapist about how I might soon be able to manage without medication. She's given me lots of ways of how I can help myself to control my feelings, how to let things go, remove myself from difficult situations and most importantly, when to ask for help. I hope I don't need the pills soon.

The boys, Jake and Ben, and their parents had a meeting with me and Mum at school. Mrs Albright was there, along with the Head teacher. Once it was all explained and their own behaviour came to light, Ben and Jake's Parents were a bit less annoyed. In fact Mrs Albright has put me on their table, so I'm a War Horse now! We work together on things and get rewards for doing just that, so it makes the others try to be so much nicer. Ben, Jake and I are actually what you might call friends now! Miss Dunbar calls us the Three Musketeers, and Jake invited me to his birthday party which was dry-slope snowboarding. It seems that I'm a natural at that; Jake and Ben even asked me for advice. I'm definitely asking them both to my party in the Autumn when we will be Year 7's and at secondary school! Maybe we'll meet up in the mornings and walk together in a chatty grown-up sort of way.

PLAY IT AGAIN SAM!

I've always found singing "do-be-do-be-do-bop" to myself reassuring in times of need, usually times of uncertainty, sometimes sadness. It just comes back to me as if it will make everything ok. Why? I don't know, maybe it's just familiar and soothing.

My Dad used to play a musical game with me. It was called 'Do This!' We used to play it when we were waiting for someone or something, in the car, or when we just had the luxury of some time alone together, which in a big family is rare. We mostly played 'Musical Do This' in the car driving along, and my Dad would use the steering-wheel to tap out his tune; I had to copy on my lap. Once it was in the A & E Department of the Childrens' Hospital in Sheffield I remember, and here his knee took the place of a drum.

David Burgess had shoved a desk over in the classroom in temper when I was ten years old. It fell smack on my foot, actually on my big toe to be exact! I was a brave soul, well-used to falling off bikes and ponies, and so returned to my seat in class, trying to ignore the pain of my throbbing toe. Much as I wanted it to go away or magically get better by itself, it wasn't going to. I hated the idea of attracting attention to myself but my sock was feeling mushy with the blood, so I knew I couldn't ignore it. I reached down and took my shoe off, only to find my white sock mostly red and the blood was still creeping up.

"Mr Gadd, I've got a problem," I said, head under the desk, arm raised to signal for help.

Mr Gadd came over, frowned and helped me up. I limped out of the classroom door with him supporting me by the elbow, and we set off down the corridor to the Headmaster's Office. It was a primary school, well a middle-school to be precise, and the Head teacher thought nothing of dealing with things like this himself. Also, having had all three of my older brothers through the school, Mr Whitestone knew my family well.

My Dad was duly called from his work-office to take me to the Casualty Department. Whilst waiting to be seen at the hospital, we played "Do This!" My Dad tapped out a tune on his lap with his hands and I had to follow. Then he would make up a 'ditty' to sing like "de diddle iddle iddle oo pa-pah."

Either way, the tap or the ditty got longer and more complex. It was a test to see if I could keep up, and it was fun. I was never a very musical child. Short of being able to play a few notes on the recorder, I couldn't play an instrument. Now, it's all I want to be able to do. I'm so envious of people who can play an instrument or sing. I would like nothing better than to be able to play the piano, the guitar or to sing in a choir.

It doesn't mean that I don't love music, because I do. I have music on wherever I am; in the car or as soon as I get home, either the radio or a CD of the moment. I spent a year in Chicago in my twenties and lapped up the Jazz and Blues music played there live in the bars. If I feel like it, I'll listen to Classical music, I love Pop music and am in awe of Rappers. I listen to the lyrics of Rap so I can try to sing it myself, and it always interests me what people are trying to say through their songs.

There was an incident in school, the same year as the 'toe' incident, which I think must have put me off exploring my love of music though. I ended up deciding that music just wasn't for me, and the following years in school therefore, I spent ignoring the very notion, as I threw myself head-long into sport instead. I knew I was good at sport, the results spoke for themselves and people praised me for my hockey and rounders skills.

The thing that put me off music at the time was this. Mrs Haydon was our music teacher and she was very, very, very strict! We used to sit for her lessons in those old-fashioned, Victorian-style rows of desks, like Victorian children. One behind the other, with gaps in-between the rows, which made it easier for her to make a bee-line up and down and reprimand any poor soul who 'wasn't doing it right'. There was a boy called Neil, I don't remember his surname and he used to drink ink. Yes ink! We all had fountain pens then, which we would fill up with ink kept in bottles in the well at the front of our desk. Neil was just finishing squeezing his fountain pen, and it filled up with the dark-blue liquid. Mrs Haydon called us to attention for the start of the music lesson, but I couldn't help but see Neil, who sat in the desk next to me, put the pen in his mouth and suck in the ink. I was completely amazed and horrified in equal measures. The result of this was for him to have very dark- blue lips, ink all around his mouth and consequently, the back of his hand, as he tried to wipe clean the evidence. I was so frightened of Mrs Haydon myself, and didn't really want Neil to be spotted doing this strange thing either. Not an ounce of good was going to come of this I thought. So I motioned to Neil quickly to wipe his mouth again.

Too late! Impending doom! Mrs Haydon had already started the lesson and I, not Neil, had been caught!

"Samantha Stevens! Stand up!"

Heat flushed my face immediately. Oh no! Please no! I was thinking, don't make me do anything bad. I stood there and the whole class was looking at me. Neil had both hands in front of his face in order to hide his 'vampire-ink mouth'. He was probably wondering if I would tell on him. How could she not have seen! The truth is I just don't think Mrs Haydon liked me; I wasn't 'musical' in her book. I didn't sing in the school choir and I didn't play in the school orchestra. But Neil did, he was actually a very good flautist.

"Samantha, I asked for your attention and clearly you would prefer to look elsewhere, and not at me!" raged Mrs Haydon.

"Therefore I would like you to sing us all a 'middle C' note."

This was such a random request in my mind. It must have been the first part of the lesson which I had obviously missed while I'd been caught up in Neil's ink-antics! It made absolutely no sense to me and I hadn't a clue what 'middle C' sounded like. Or maybe this was just a standard punishment that she knew people like me couldn't action. I had no choice but to give it a go and hey! I thought there was even a chance that I could strike lucky... So off I went:

"Laaaa"

"Too high" she snapped.

"Laaaaa"

"Still too high"

"Laa"

"Too low"

Her pleasure in proving a point was obvious. Added to that I could hear the stifled, half-embarrassed, half-delighted snickering of some of my class-mates. Neil just stayed in the corner of my eye with his hands over his face. I think he was shaking, and to this day I don't know if that would have been through terror or amusement.

"Sit down!" shouted Mrs Haydon at me, happy now I had been humiliated and she had made her point to both me and the rest of the class.

Neil raised his hand and asked to go to the toilet. He used the chance to clean himself up, but I could still see the ink round his mouth when he got back, so why couldn't she? Also, didn't she think it might be bad for him?

Anyway, whatever. But that was my moment of persuading myself that music just wasn't for me! What a shame.

My father, Mr Whitestone, Mr Gadd and the infamous Mrs Haydon are all dead now but their actions and their words still live on. People can leave a lasting impression on other peoples' lives; parents and teachers have such power to determine a child's self-esteem. Sometimes they don't even realise.

All I care to remember is my Dad impersonating James Cagney and saying to me "Play it again Sam!" It was fun and to be fair I did get better at the 'diddley's!'

My Dad wasn't a music teacher but secretly I think he would have made a very good one!

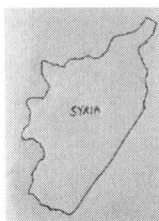

SYRIA

"Everybody up! Rise and shine! Come on sleepy-heads, it's a beautiful day out there!"

It was Mick's ever-cheerful voice. 6 am at Ullswater Outdoor Education Centre in Cumbria. Bleary-eyed, Mohammed turned onto his stomach, pulling his starched-white regulation sheets over his shoulders. He sandwiched his head between the two flat pillows and tried to ignore the world.

Hummmphs, groans and stretching noises escaped the reluctant bodies of his teenage peers around the room. The dormitory slept six and Mohammed only really knew one of the other boys. The two of them had just started sixth-form together at Canterbury School in Kent. Mohammed had been fortunate to get a place there, he knew that, but he was an intelligent young man and showed great promise; quite an achievement, considering the life-journey he had made so far.

He had come to Britain's shores an orphan, rescued from deportation by a deeply empathetic support-worker for Syrian refugees, called Kate Dunstan. She had been called to Mohammed at around 8 pm one night by an alert, originally from a fisherman, at Kingsdown beach, not too far from Dover. She found Mohammed dazed, confused and exhausted. He had half-swum, half been dragged to the shore in the darkness and had shivered and crawled his way to safety on the shale beach, away from the unrepentant sea. The others had not been so lucky.

An emergency call had come in on Kate's mobile 'phone Just as she was leaving the terminal office at Dover. She accepted the call and the consequent errand of mercy, without hesitation. A fisherman at Kingsdown had just finished-up securing his nets and fishing boat on the beach as twilight turned to dark. He had spotted a figure every now and again bobbing up and down on every new wave, pushing the human-form closer to the shore with each dark pulse. When Mohammed clawed his way to safety, the fisherman realised his eyes had not been deceived and there on the moonlight-bathed shore lay the body of a young man. Mohammed was quite limp and the fisherman did what he could, pushing down on Mohammed's weary back, urgently trying to rid his lungs of the salty water he was struggling to splutter. Before long he was able to raise Mohammed to a sitting-position and he leant forwards, elbows on knees. He was going to be ok. The fisherman wrapped his coat around Mohammed's shoulders and sat down alongside him on the uncomfortable shale.

Several 'phone calls and forty-five minutes later Kate had arrived. She knew she should contact the police and the border police at Dover but all that could wait. Kate thanked the fisherman for his kindness and initially intended getting Mohammed checked out at Buckland hospital just outside Dover. Mohammed had walked quite capably up the beach and had gratefully accepted the bottle of water and bourbon biscuits that Kate had in the car. He was shivering but other than that she felt he'd survive. She ran the engine and put the heater on. The fisherman's coat was still around Mohammed's shoulders as he had insisted they keep it, and in doing so had restored some of Kate's faith in human kindness. 'There are still some good people', she thought as she frantically dialled her friends.

Kate's friends lived nearby on a small farm in Bridge, a village about half an hour away. Maybe if she could take Mohammed there, get him warm, dry and safe... then she could consider where to go with this next. She knew that as soon as the police were involved, the border-force, the home-office, the likelihood was that Mohammed would be deported. It looked very much like he was Syrian and goodness only knows what happened to the rest of his family and friends, Kate thought. No news yet of other refugees turning up via the ocean, she considered. She would keep this quiet for Mohammed's sake for the time being.

Kate was a humanitarian of the first order. She spent several years abroad in her twenties working for the Red Cross in Bali to support the victims of the 2004 tsunami. When things were looking like they were finally improving and aid to the area was more consistent, Kate had been called back to the UK to help with Somalian, Afghanistani, Eastern European and more recently, Syrian refugees.

Which way to jump now? Kate decided she couldn't bear to let Mohammed go back to his home in war-torn Syria, he had made a mammoth effort to get free already, and who knows what he'd already lost in doing so. She looked at him, still exhausted and withdrawn in the darkness of the car. She knew no Arabic and so far communication had consisted of gestures and intonation in her voice, mixed with the British Sign Language she had learnt in University many years ago. She was actually still quite proficient at sign language, Mohammed however, was not. Kate spoke many languages fluently; French, Thai, German, Spanish, but not Arabic.

'Hold-on though', thought Kate to herself as she pressed the dial button to be connected, 'Donald spent time as an archaeologist in Northern Africa, if I remember rightly. Surely he will speak Arabic...'

Judy answered almost immediately.

"Kate! Darling! How are you? And what's the occasion for you calling on such a dark night, are you ok?"

"Well not really Judy, actually!" Kate replied honestly and was so relieved to hear her friend's familiar, comforting tones.

"Can I come over? I'm just leaving the beach at Kingsdown and I have someone with me. Judy, it's a long story..."

"Of course Kate, don't explain. We'll aim to see you in half an hour or so, and you can tell us all about it then."

Judy and Donald were old friends and right now Kate needed them. Kate had helped many people in their hour of need but always in a professional manner and through the proper channels. This time was going to be tough and she needed some help.

Sitting at their old pine table, lamps low and flickering in the farmhouse kitchen, Kate got her first proper look at Mohammed away from the darkness of the car. She took in his tall frame and his jet-black hair which was plastered to his head from being wet and then drying without being touched. She knew he was Syrian from his skin-tone and his brown sorrowful eyes. She guessed he was around 16 years of age.

Kate introduced Mohammed to Judy and Donald saying they were friends and would help. He seemed to understand. Then Donald spoke in Arabic and Mohammed perked up; they had a conversation, quite easily it seemed to Kate and Judy, and relief poured over Kate.

Donald got the story.

"You have to go through the proper channels with this Kate," said Donald. It's your job on the line here. He's a refugee and at present, an illegal immigrant."

Donald told Kate and Judy the whole sad story of Mohammed. He didn't know where his family were. Their boat had capsized many hours ago and he had swum for his life, being unable to find them in the water. Everyone had been panicking, Donald explained, and thinking his Mum, Dad and younger brother would follow suit, Mohammed had set off swimming for the shore. He thought he would alert the authorities once on land but he was too weak and confused; he thought he was dying. One thing led to another and he thought he'd better stay quiet as he would probably be arrested.

"The fact remains though Kate that we need to tell the police he's here."

"Okay fine. If that's what you think, but personally I haven't the heart to send him back to a war in Syria, where he probably has no family Donald. Look, give me a bit of time," Kate implored, "so I can 'phone the guys in Dover and see if anything has come up with the boat Mohammed was on."

Kate made the call outside the farmhouse door. What shocked her was that she hadn't expected to be told so quickly, so easily, so abruptly, that Mohammed's world was about to crash even further. The sea and air rescue crews had salvaged one hundred and more bodies from the English

Channel. All dead. Mohammed now belonged to no-one, had no-one and that stark reality was about to hit him. In immigration terms he was now a 'separated child.' Kate went back into the kitchen to deliver the heart-breaking news.

Donald put it to Mohammed the best way he could but there is no good way to tell someone that everyone they love in the world has gone. A cruel outcome to what was a break for freedom from the misery and potential death in Syria. Any chance had been a better option than the life they were living. Mohammed and his family had spent the last few weeks in hiding, with little food, little water and constant bomb attacks from the Russians in support of the Syrian government. Not aimed at them of course, but ironically innocent Syrian people were more and more commonly the victims. Just caught up in it all.

"Tragic, just tragic." Judy spoke softly and placed her hand on Mohammed's shoulder. He was crying now, sobbing, a broken man. He and his family had been so close to escaping and had been willing to risk everything they found once they made it to Britain. Hoping above hope that they would be able to stay and make a life here.

"Surely you can pull some strings Kate." Judy's sad face said it all.

Donald stared at his feet, wondering if he might find the answer there. The reality was this had become their problem now though. All of them. They were in it with Mohammed and all were bound by an overwhelming sadness.

"I'll need a few days," said Kate, "Is there any way Mohammed could stay here with you in the meantime? Just so they can't physically get hold of him?"

"Sure," Donald and Judy spoke in unison and Kate felt she was half-way there. At least he would be safe, warm and protected for the short-term. Another bonus of course would be that Mohammed could speak with Donald in his own language.

Over 4,000 refugees from Sudan, Iran, Eritrea and Syria had been rejected by the UK government last year, thought Kate. The majority of these being asylum seekers like Mohammed, due to war in their own country. But surely his position would be strengthened now that he was officially an orphan.

Kate left early the next morning to drive to work in Dover. It was April and the rain was thrashing down on her windscreen, her wipers working double-time to clear it.

"April-showers!" she mused, "more like someone throwing a bucket of water on the windscreen!"

She had left a note for Mohammed on the kitchen table, tucked under the vase of daffs which she had stared at without knowing, most of last night. 'Mohammed, see you in a few days, Kate x', the note read. She knew Donald would translate it and although it didn't say much, at least it was a message, something to say she cared.

Kate dashed from car-park to office, her hands keeping the hood of her anorak on her head. 'April showers' and didn't she just know it! She peeled off her waterproof and hung it on the coat-stand in the foyer to dry; 'quite a retro coat-stand' for this place she thought, with its dark-wooden curved arms, each punctuated with a brightly coloured ball on which to hang your coat. 'Bit like an over-turned spider,' she concluded in her own mind.

She dashed up the stairs, wondering what this was going to sound like to her boss.

"Kate! Good morning! You look a little wet! How's things with you? Oh, and before you start, great news! David Cameron has pledged support for 3,000 child refugees in the UK, immediately and asylum for a total of 20,000people over the next five years! Terribly sad about those in the channel last night, dreadful shame, poor things."

Kate plonked into the seat opposite Marilyn, Marilyn Hooper, a hard and fast boss, but a heart of gold, and she had just given Kate the best news in the world. Relief spread over her like a warm blanket, comforting and safe. Kate felt like crying there and then, but she had learnt over the years that it's not the way forward when professionalism is needed. If Kate had cried for every poor soul that she had come across, she would be useless by now. No, she always stayed strong, maintained a clear mind and just dealt with it, which was what made her so good at her job.

"Oh Marilyn, that certainly is wonderful news! In fact that's what I need to talk to you about. I may not have gone about what I'm going to tell you, in exactly the right way, but I think you will understand why, and I can't see that any harm has been done." Kate explained.

She relayed the events of the previous evening carefully, bit by very precise bit. Marilyn nodded with understanding but looked concerned.

"Kate, I know you, I've worked with you for many years now and we've done some very good work on behalf of the Red Cross for humanity between us. We've saved many lives and certainly improved the quality of life for countless others. I know you truly care and I can only support your intentions for this young man. So know that I fully support you and I will do whatever I can. Take today to find appropriate accommodation for Mohammed, a possible school, doctors, dentist, what-have-you. Meanwhile, I will give this my personal attention in applying for asylum for him. Tell me what personal details you know of him..."

"Well so far very little," admitted Kate. "It sounds certain that his parents and brother were picked up last night from the sea and are dead. Donald is with him now, I'll ask him to get details from Mohammed, of his age, date of birth, any other possible family either here or in Syria."

After an hour or so Donald called Kate back. He had as much info as he could get from Mohammed, but it was early days and he still seemed in shock, Donald explained. Mohammed hadn't eaten this morning but they were hoping he would have some lunch. He had at least had a fruit-tea of Judy's. He was quiet and sobbed from time to time, only to be expected really.

"What do you need the info for Kate? Are you making any headway? ", asked Donald cautiously.

"Well, it's needed for his asylum application firstly. I also need it to be able to find him emergency accommodation, school, doctors etc. The sooner we sort this, the better his case is for staying Donald."

"Oh but Kate, listen, Judy and I have been talking and we would like Mohammed to stay here! Is there any chance he can stay here with us? Call it fate or whatever, but we feel you came to us with Mohammed for a reason. He's a dear chap and Jude and I want to do our bit."

"Donald, it's more than a bit! It's at least the next two years..."

"Yes, well count us in because ours have both left home now. There's a room waiting upstairs for him and we'd love to help out with school, college and all that stuff."

Kate was overwhelmed.

"Oh Donald, I can't thank you enough. It looks like we're going to be ok; Cameron has pledged support for 3,000 child refugees today and Mohammed is still classed as a child refugee, sad as that is, but I think that is a good sign that he'll be able to stay. If you and Jude are willing, I think that would seal it! Thank-you, thank-you, thank-you Donald!"

With that she hung up.

Mohammed duly attended the sixth-form at Canterbury school in Kent, just twenty minutes' drive from his new home in Bridge. He had already missed a significant amount of school but he was clearly a bright lad. Donald said he would put in time with him at home, although his assessment tests on arrival at the school bode well. Mohammed would study Geography A Level, and a BTEC in PE and Sport.

It was at Canterbury School that Mohammed met his new friend James who was with him now in Ullswater. They were studying the BTEC in PE together, and as part of that they were studying Outdoor Pursuits. Hence the trip to the Lake District.

"Come on! Breakfast is served and it's now or never! If you want food before we head-off, you'll be in the dining room in under a minute!" barked Mick.

"Ok, okaaaay. Let me through the door James!"

Mohammed's English was coming on leaps and bounds. Being thrown into English school-life, surrounded by his new language, he was picking it up daily. Judy was helping him also, and the fact that she was non-Arabic speaking, gave him no choice but to progress.

"Only English, all lesson," was Judy's rule.

Mohammed went from serious to smiling and occasionally to laughing and joking with her. Usually, it was his own mispronunciations that Mohammed laughed at, once Judy had modelled the correct version for him and he realised his error. She taught him loads of useful vocabulary related to clothes, shopping, school, music, sport, food and money. He would listen carefully while she described photos and pictures. He copied her model of the words he needed to learn. Honing in on the grammar was the tough part., but at least Mohammed would be well-taught.

The first full day at Ullswater Outdoor Education Centre was a mixture of fun, challenge and sore muscles from hiking. Mick gave the students a map, divided them into two groups and set a final meeting-point.

"Sounds simple enough," said James.

"I'm not so sure" Mohammed replied, "because don't these lines here mean hills?"

"Ah yes," interjected Amanda, one of the girls in their group, "they're contours, and when they're tight like that it means mountains!"

"Well done that group," said Mick, "some brains amongst you! Before you set-off, let's translate the map together."

The next few hours were spent orientating themselves with the map; finding N, E, S and W on the compass and varying degrees NE, SW etc. They identified where the rivers, streams and lakes were, and what the key stood for. Mick felt that once the students understood a grid reference, the scale in miles to the cm and compass directions, he was happy for them to start their journey. They would walk for an hour and then stop for lunch, finally meeting up around 4 pm at the Inn in Troutbeck. They would then all walk the three miles or so back to the Centre by road together.

Everything looked so beautiful to Mohammed, so rich, so well. It was late in the Autumn but still the colours lingered, the purple and yellow heather, the bracken and ferns still very-much green. The tinges of brown were merely the inevitable testament to the winter beginning to take hold. It was drizzling with rain, but Mohammed didn't mind, as the others chuntered away to themselves, moaning about feeling wet and cold, he felt content. Mohammed opened his mouth to catch the rain, savouring it as if he was tasting his own freedom. He had been in the UK now for seven months, but already the dreadful memories of his dry, war-torn home in Syria were becoming harder to remember. Maybe his mind just didn't want to remember.

Sometimes he woke at night still, sitting bolt upright in bed; night terrors where the noise of the gun-fire and the threat of gas-bombs were all too real. He then remembered his family and the realisation came again that they were no longer alive. Then he would think of how lucky he was now, of Donald, of Judy and Kate, which enabled him to get back to a calmer sleep. The sweats would stop and peace be restored in him until morning came. Mohammed had seen a social worker a few times and a family support worker also, but everyone agreed he was going to be fine where he was placed, with Judy and Donald. He had a good school and he was faring well.

It was on the second day at Ullswater that a situation arose which Mohammed found hard to deal with however. The students were to be faced with a challenge on the water. This began with raft-building. In pairs they had to tie together a raft of logs, complete with plastic containers for buoyancy. They were supplied with long sticks for 'punts', and were expected to build a raft good enough to navigate the bright-orange buoy which was about 100 metres from the shore. Added to that was the fact that it was a race.

"Around the buoy and first pair back are the winners!" announced Mick.

Mohammed was filled with dread but didn't want to recount his whole, horrible story of the English Channel to Mick, especially not in front of all the others. No, maybe he could do this. 'After-all it is about challenging yourself,' he thought. It was just that this challenge was going to test him far more than the others. James knew something of what had happened to Mohammed, but Mick had no idea of his circumstances, only that he was a refugee from Syria.

The two lads, James and Mohammed worked quickly together against the clock.

"Just like Huckleberry Finn!" laughed James, although the quip was a bit lost on Mohammed. They laid the logs out in the shallow water as the floating would help when they were fixing them together.

"Smart move!" Mohammed said to James' idea. James was on a roll!

"You bunch all the shorter logs together side by side Mohammed, and I'll get six long logs to go across them, three under and three on top. We'll sandwich the short ones that way. They lashed the logs together securely at every meeting-point with the twine they'd been given, James fortunately remembering his half-hitches and clove-hitches from his Scouting days. Mohammed looked on impressed, and did his bit by fastening four large plastic containers, threading the blue twine through their handles, at each corner of the raft.

"That should help keep us afloat." Mohammed stood back, hands on hips, admiring their creation.

"Right, let's go!" announced James, patting Mohammed on the shoulder encouragingly.

They pushed the raft out into the lake as far as they could and scrambled on-board.

"Oh no! We forgot the poles for punting!" James jumped in and waded back to shore just as the next pair had completed their raft.

"Quick James!" shouted Mohammed, "or they'll over-take us!"

James picked up the long sticks and scurried back into the water, pushing them along the surface in front of him, towards Mohammed who was crouching and beckoning from the raft. Mohammed took one of the poles and shakily went to stand at the front of the raft while James managed to haul himself on and take up the rear. 'Thank goodness for wet-suits', thought James. The lake was freezing and he would have had some terrible scrapes by now, from hauling himself onto the raft, without the extra protection.

If they got this right; kept each other balanced and their poles found the bottom of the lake in unison, so that they could push together, nobody would catch them. They were too unsteady though and James, losing his balance, toppled and fell in. With James floundering around, Mohammed started to get flashbacks of the large motorised dinghy he, his family and a hundred or so others had been crammed into for two days. Then the night itself, all the people shouting, screaming in the water.

James was back on board the raft now, they were still ahead and just about to round the orange buoy but not quite turning for home. They were still facing out towards the vast lake which stretched beyond.

Mohammed froze on hands and knees, a solid lump of fear and unable to move.

"Mohammed mate! Are you okay? Come-on! They're catching us!" rallied James from the back.

"I can't do it man, I'm sorry, I just can't!" Mohammed tried to explain, now not just trembling, but his whole body shaking uncontrollably. He managed to lie down flat on his front and grip the edges of the raft for all he was worth. His pole had long-since gone, and was now bobbing a few metres away on the little waves created by the wind.

"Mate, are you okay?" he could hear James asking again, but he couldn't answer. He was paralysed by fear and he just wanted 'this' and the memories to stop.

Somehow James managed to single-handedly punt them back to the shore but they were over-taken by everyone of course, and came in last. Mohammed felt he owed everyone, well maybe Mick and James, a proper explanation. That evening he 'phoned Kate. She was always at the ready to help him, and was still a close family friend of Judy and Donald. She asked to speak to Mick and explained the situation, how she had found Mohammed that night at Kingsdown beach, and how his family had died. Mick told Mohammed that he had done so well, facing a difficult situation out on the lake today, giving it a go and trying to persevere for James. Mick said he was proud of him.

Mohammed told Mick that he felt he should explain to James, which he did. The other students were all outside after dinner playing football on the grass, overlooking the spectacular lake. They even paused their game every now and again to admire the breath-taking view.

Mohammed asked James if he would stay behind for a few minutes. They sat in the common-room, on red plastic chairs facing each other, Mohammed sitting upright, wringing his hands nervously and James was leaning forward, incredulous at Mohammed's story.

Hard lessons for Mohammed, but a few years on, as time has passed, the memories come less-often. As for Ullswater, he received a special award from Mick for 'grit and determination'. There were plenty of other awards given of course, but his meant the world to him.

Mohammed is still friends with James even now and sees him when he can. James became an Outdoor Ed. Instructor in Barnstaple, Devon. Mohammed, is also now in his 20's and works with Kate and Marilyn for the Red Cross, supporting refugees. He's been through it all himself and is a great addition to the team. It was the most worthwhile job he could think of doing and naturally drifted into it. He sees Judy and Donald whenever he can, and being their one and only refugee, he owes them so much.

Donald just says "Mohammed, to know you is to love you!"

CONCUSSION!

I was always the one to get reprimanded in the back of the car as my father was driving along! He would suddenly snap, having had enough, which is exactly what he said.

"Enough is enough! Stop-it now or we'll all be killed in a car-accident if you don't calm down!"

It sounded general enough but it seemed it was me he eye-balled in his rear-view mirror. Those were the days when seatbelts were not compulsory and kids took liberties in the car, messing-around. My brothers were over-joyed as I took the blame. They all shuffled up somehow to avoid his eye-contact, and as I was the youngest I always seemed to 'catch it'. So many times I remember saying "but it wasn't me!" Maybe they were just older and 'smarter'.

I'm not saying it's acceptable either, it most certainly isn't; regardless of what size family you come from or your position in that family. It would probably be considered as being bullied now, and quite rightly, children are encouraged to make it known when they feel they are being bullied. It's not okay on any level but it's the way it was then for me, and it's part of my story.

We lived in Sheffield, South Yorkshire, and every holiday possible, we packed up the car, a silver Escort Estate; parents and four kids, (until my baby sister was born), and headed for the coast near Filey. My parents had bought a bungalow at Reighton Gap, so we could go whenever we wanted. Quite often my father would drive us there, stay a little while, and then head back to Sheffield for work. After my sister was born, my Mum would drive her own car, just her and the baby, with most of the 'supplies' we needed for our stay by the sea. It was an added bonus then, as when my father had taken one car back to Sheffield, she could still run us around.

So, my Dad had the four older ones in the car on his own. Not easy. We travelled in convoy as far as possible, but sometimes my Mum would get separated, and it didn't really matter. It was a long journey and often we would call in at Driffield for fish and chips, which was something to look forward to. The best part of the journey was when we came into Reighton Gap, there were three huge 'humps' in the road, and I mean huge! My Dad would literally drive up one side, like the side of a mountain, and down the other side, like steering a ship up and down tall waves in a storm with a crew shouting Whoahhhh!!, every time we went up, and every time we came down! Captain Pugwash, eat your heart out!

The bungalow had a very long counter which ran along a very long window, and it's where we all ate breakfast. The view was of other bungalows across the way and then the sea beyond. I loved these holidays as we were given quite a lot of freedom. The road that passed along the bottom of our garden was more of a grassy track really, so cars were never a problem as they had to traverse the ridges, grooves and potholes in the grass very slowly. Being a keen sportsperson, I was never happier than when I was playing cricket or football on the lawn with my three older brothers, and to this day I am quite an adept player of both. They took me into their games as if I was one of the boys, but being the youngest, it was quite a rough time for me! I was also allowed to go exploring around Primrose Valley and down the 'gill' which was a wooded ravine leading down to the beach. The only rule was that at least one of the boys had to be with me, which was fair enough seeing as I was only seven years old when we first got the bungalow!

The other amazing thing about these holidays was that I loved riding ponies, and I got to do plenty of that. One of my brothers, Aidan, was the same. So, especially in the summer holidays, but really any chance we got, we would spend day after day at the riding school in Hunmanby. I loved the smell of the stables there, and as soon as Mum dropped us off we would wander into the yard to be engulfed by a heavenly scent. It was a mixture of horses, leather, saddle-soap, linseed oil and manure! My brother, next one up in age from me, was a bit of a superstar at the riding school. He was in his early teens, a good rider and had long hair which was very trendy then. He knew the girls all liked him as well. Quite often there was a bunch of girls his age helping out at the stables; mucking out, cleaning tack, leading the younger riders on a rein, feeding the horses or just doing whatever needed doing.

Many times I saw them having a joke with him, giving him a leg-up onto his horse, which he gratefully accepted, only to be thrown over the other side. They were cool with me being around as I was harmless enough, I was Aidan's sister and quite a brave little rider to boot. Hunmanby, by the way was called so by the Early Danes. They actually named it 'Hundemanebi' which means 'the Farmstead of the Houndsman' apparently, and I rather fancied I could ride horses like a Dane!

During the summer there was always a gymkhana which my brother and I really looked forward to. Sometimes these gymkhanas were proper Pony Club events for the area, other times they were just 'in-house' end of summer events for the riding school. My brother and I had the proper Pony Club tie and badge and brought them with us on our holiday, along with jodhpurs and a white cotton school-shirt, in case it was the more formal event. We looked smart then, all kitted out with our Jodhpur boots on and black velvet-covered riding hats. Sometimes we entered gymkhana events together, like the fancy dress event where we would disappear into the tack-room to change and re-emerge as Laurel and Hardy for example. Mostly we were entered into different age groups though, taking part in events such as the 'Round the World' race which involved circum-navigating your pony while sitting on them by spinning your legs around. There were lots and lots of relay races in teams, as well as show-jumping.

My favourite pony was Sunrise, she was a palomino and I thought she was just beautiful. She was a chipper little pony and not afraid to jump, and she was best-buddies with Bambi, a male pony and a 'grey'. These two ponies were virtually inseparable and would push other ponies out of the way if they got in-between them. They were always nose to tail consequently in the riding school arena. Sunrise had such a pretty face, with a white mop of a forelock falling down over her chestnut-colour eyes and a white 'star' on her golden face. Her body was golden with a slight dapple-effect on her hind-quarters. She also had the most elegant legs, and a lovely nature. It made me happy to be allowed to pick the mud or sand out of her hooves as part of getting her ready for a gymkhana and applying varnish to her hooves. She looked so shiny and pretty, and I'm sure she used to smile!

One particular summer and gymkhana, my Mum had, as usual, made me promise to wear my riding hat at all times. I had agreed just to make her feel better, which was stupid because I should have agreed and stuck to it, in order to keep myself safe. My brother and his friends, had a very cavalier attitude towards wearing riding hats; it was so much 'cooler' <u>not</u> to wear one, so they rarely did. There weren't really any hard and fast rules then either, but obviously the people in charge would rather you wear one.

This particular summer I was nine years old and still just small enough to ride Sunrise in the less formal gymkhana that the riding school were having. I felt so lucky to get her as she was indeed my favourite. I put my foot in the stirrup and mounted her quite neatly by myself. I loved her saddle, it was old and so supple that it moulded to Sunrise's back and my knees like a warm toffee. Sunrise smelt heavenly, all saddle-soap, varnish and horse! I liked my stirrups quite long as it made me feel more balanced, easier to stay on really. The instructor, Jane, came round to check all our saddle-girths and make sure we were 'good to go.' She also hitched my stirrups up one more notch; "just so you don't clang your feet on the jumps," she explained.

I felt a little bit unstable, but kept the stirrups at the length Jane had suggested. The gymkhana was great fun; young people laughing and calling out encouragingly to each other, ponies doing their best and competing with each other. They were enjoying it as much as we were! The fun events were over bar the final team relay which always came at the very end, after the show-jumping. I had been taking part in the fun events without my riding hat because there was always a lot of jumping on and off your pony, for example travelling backwards along the pony's back, sliding off their tail-end before hurrying back round to re-mount. It had been easier not to wear it.

So, show-jumping next. I should have put my riding hat on then, but nobody told me to and my Mum wasn't there to see. Besides I wanted to be like the older kids and so threw caution to the wind. It was me and Sunrise next to go. I leaned forwards and whispered to her:

"Come-on girl, let's do this!"

Squeezing her hard with my calves and giving her 'her head', we sped off towards the first jump. They weren't too high and Sunrise had done this a million times before so I was confident. We sailed over that first criss-crossed jump and turned for the double-width fence which made the little pony stretch. She didn't think she could make it for some reason and changed her mind half-way over, just stumbling into the whole thing at speed, as it had been too late for her to back-out of the situation. Sunrise ejected me over her head and I was dispatched neatly onto <u>my</u> head in the sandy 'ring'. I just remember the clatter and not much more. People were helping me up and I remember some others helping Sunrise who seemed to be ok.

I was not ok. All I could see was 'green', everything and everyone looked green. I was dazed and confused, felt sick and my head and neck really hurt. My Mum was called to take me to Driffield Hospital where I stayed the night. When I was allowed home the next day it was under strict instruction for me to lie-down and rest; 'concussion' they said.

My Mum was as kind as she could be under the circumstances, as I had gone against her wishes by not wearing a riding-hat. It was one of those times though that made me realise that maybe sometimes adults really do know best.

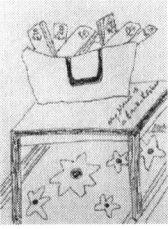

MY MUM IS A BANK-ROBBER!

"What are the chances of you getting out of bed today Simon?"

"Oh I'd say about 50:50 Mum, why?" Simon groaned.

"Well, because I know it's the weekend but I need you to help me with something please," replied his mother.

"Erm, depends what it is..."

"Well, actually it's a bank-robbery," his Mum said over her shoulder as she left him in peace.

"Yeah, right Mum!" Simon said, slightly amused, and then turned over, pulling the duvet tight around him to catch some more sleep.

It was about 2 o'clock in the afternoon when he finally surfaced from the bedroom. Sloping downstairs in his dressing-gown, Simon wandered into the kitchen-come-dining room-come-living room. There on the dining table was a hold-all, and it was stuffed, and I mean stuffed full of notes. Bank-notes, like... money notes!

Suddenly Simon was wide-awake! He circled the table like a shark, bobbing up and down at the same time, to see what exactly was going on in that bag! Maybe it was a mirage and if he looked from a different angle it would disappear, just like water in the desert. He could smell it! It was definitely the smell of money, sort of musty but fresh at the same time; a papery, inky, wealthy smell.

A key turned in the front-door and Simon ducked down behind the table. 'Oh dear God,' he thought, 'what if... what if that's not Mum at the door?!'

Whoever it was, they were struggling with the key in the lock and that gave Simon just enough time to make a sharp exit. He shot up the stairs, taking them two at a time as quietly, but as fast as he could. His dressing-gown swished around him as he hadn't bothered to tie it, which would have required far too much effort. He stood on the landing where he was close enough to his bedroom door to run and hide, but where he also had a view of the downstairs hall, and just inside the kitchen-dining room. The voices he heard were those of his Mum and his Uncle, Mum's brother, Ralph. They were arguing:

"Well I had to put it in <u>something</u>, didn't I? Honestly Ralph! You're such a prude sometimes!"

'Oh my goodness!' Simon remembered what his Mum had said now, the last thing she said as she went out of his bedroom this morning; she was going to rob a bank! This is ridiculous, Mum's Head of the kitchen at the local primary school, people like that don't rob banks!

It was half-term, which was why his Mum was around this week. She'd been going on for years about 'tightening our belts' now that Dad had left, but rob a bank? No. Surely not.

"Maggie," countered Ralph, "you could have been a bit more subtle, do you want people coming after you for <u>that</u> or something?"

"Maybe you're right," she replied, "but I just wanted to get it all, and as quickly as possible. I've never had a lot of money Ralph, especially not lately. I didn't even know what that much money looked like! Plus I wanted Simon to see it as well, then I could put it back perhaps?"

'Put it back!' exclaimed Simon to himself, hoping he didn't just voice that out loud. 'What sort of robber is she for Heaven's sake?'

"Maybe I'll just take enough for that moped he's after, and for a holiday for us all in the sun? Then I'll take it back, his Mum continued, she was

63

really on a roll now and Simon couldn't believe his ears. 'All that time Mum's spent telling me to be honest! Just look at her! Unbelievable!'

Simon thought back to the times his Mum had insisted on him being honest. Like for example, when he had tried all the chocolates in her Milk Tray selection that one Christmas. He must've only been about four years old. He bit into nearly all of them and left half of the ones he didn't like in the box, (Turkish-delight, coconut, toffee caramel and the coffee ones which were especially gross!). He'd never eaten a coffee-chocolate since! Mum had gone to offer them round on Christmas afternoon, when the Queen was on the telly. Mortified she was. She said it wasn't the fact he'd done it particularly, more the fact that he hadn't told her. She made him own up and apologise in front of everyone, and Simon was embarrassed just thinking about it.

Then there was the time he had 'borrowed' some money from her dressing-table drawer when he was about twelve and his Mum was in hospital. Uncle Ralph had been staying at theirs to look after him and Simon was asked to go and play Crazy Golf with his buddies. He hadn't wanted to tap his uncle for the money and assumed Mum wouldn't mind lending it. The problem was, he forgot to tell her, and when she discovered it missing wouldn't believe that he just forgot to mention it. Awkward!

If Simon had learnt one thing about living with his Mum, it was to tell her about everything, to tell her even if it seemed unnecessary, and not to let himself forget. It was a bit alien to him, as he didn't always want to communicate, it didn't come naturally to him as a teenager but it was important to Mum, so therefore, now, he tried.

"If there are two things I can't abide," she would say, "its secrets and dishonesty."

Simon found it quite exhausting to share everything he did and thought or said, all the time, but had realized it necessary for his happiness in the long-run.

So, how come, has she now done something so big and so dishonest, and completely gone against her own words? Simon felt let-down. Disappointed. Well, if she wanted openness then the shoe was about to be on the other foot. He tiptoed back to his bedroom and then made it look as if he'd just got up. Striding out of bed and tying his dressing-gown as though he'd just put it on, he closed the bedroom door noisily behind him. He made sure his footsteps could be heard across the landing and down the stairs, and even gave a little cough half-way down so they'd know he was on his way.

The hold-all with all the money in had gone from the dining table, and Ralph was sitting quietly at the other end of the room, reading a newspaper by the window. Mum had her back to Simon as she poured cereal into a bowl, then faffed around with the kettle in the kitchen-area.

"Morning Simon! Or should I say Good Afternoon?! So, what are you going to do with yourself this beautiful half-term day? Ralph's here, we've just been shopping together for some things for lunch. Here's your cereal!"

Maggie still had her back to him and was making a steaming-hot cup of tea for Uncle Ralph, coffee for herself. The sun streamed in through the kitchen window in front of her and made her look like a dark shadow standing there, 'like Darth Vader himself' thought Simon. 'Yes, a black figure of dishonesty, that's fitting.' He really was hurt now, because whatever it was, they were definitely keeping it from him. This was almost too hard though he felt, challenging adults and their honesty. The worst part was that his own Mum was now a thief, not just of a 'fiver' from a dressing-table drawer, but a big thief, like Ronnie Biggs and the Great Train Robbery, or something.

The police would be here soon, surely. Why was Uncle Ralph so calm? What was wrong with him? Have they done a 'Bonnie and Clyde' and they're planning on sharing the loot?

Simon sat quietly at the table, pushing the cereal around his bowl. 'This surely is a dream', he puzzled, 'a flipping nightmare more like, please let me wake up in a minute! If I wake up now, I promise never to sleep late again!' he thought.

Mum had joined Ralph by the window and was perched on the edge of his comfy chair. That's another thing she always told Simon, "don't sit on the arm of the chair, you'll break it!"

Simon wasn't stupid, he knew adults did things they weren't meant to as well, that they weren't perfect. After-all his Dad had left with that twitty-woman who was his secretary a few years ago. He had signed some vows with Mum promising 'in sickness and in health, to love and to cherish, 'til death us do part', hadn't he?

Simon felt sorry for Mum for that. Dad's new girlfriend tottered around on silly heels and wore far too much make-up for Simon's liking; caked-on it was! Part of him just felt relieved that he didn't have to give her a peck on the cheek like he did Grandma. Imagine! He'll probably have to go and live with them now, or maybe Grandma, when the police come to take Mum and Ralph away.

Maggie was calmly pointing things out on her 'phone to Ralph. She was so in love with her iPhone 6. Simon had bought her a new green case for it, (green being her favourite colour). It was a rubbery case to stop it slipping down in-between the cushions of the sofa, which was quite often what happened. She was emoji-mad, and sent more pictures than actual words to anyone. Simon didn't get that! She also once sent LOL to one of her friends whose cat had just died, thinking she was sending lots of love, when actually was laughing out loud, which made him cringe at the thought.

Simon tried chewing some of his cereal, but it wasn't 'happening', he was definitely off his food. Being unable to bear this 'falseness' and deceit any longer, he took the bull by the horns.

"Mum, I saw a bag of money on the table."

That was it, it was out now. Caught! 'So who's the big honesty guy now? Me, of course!' Simon congratulated himself.

His words floated towards them both, like black clouds on a mission of Hell. That was it; cat out of the bag, so to speak. Mum looked at Ralph. Ralph looked at Mum. They both smiled. Well! The audacity of it-they're even proud of themselves. As he waited for a response, Simon looked beyond them and out over the hedge in the front garden to check for 'cops', blue flashing-lights, black helmets; all that stuff. No-one here yet!

"Mum?" Simon was getting upset now. He could actually feel tears welling-up and felt that at any moment they could all come spurting out of his eyes like in the cartoons, like jets from a hose.

"We were going to tell you Simon...It was a surprise."

"What? Tell me what?"

"That I've won twenty thousand pounds, that's what!" shrieked his Mum as she started dancing around the room.

"I did ask you to get up and help this morning!" she said.

Ralph stayed seated, but turned to look at Simon, laughing.

"It's true Simon, she's won twenty grand on the Lottery! A hundred thousand, shared between five people who had the same numbers! National Lottery put it in her bank account, and she's only gone and drawn the whole lot out this morning!"

19369488R00040

Printed in Poland
by Amazon Fulfillment
Poland Sp. z o.o., Wrocław